THE LINK

THE LINK

by Alan E. Nourse

It was nearly sundown when Ravdin eased the ship down into the last slow arc toward the Earth's surface. Stretching his arms and legs, he tried to relax and ease the tension in his tired muscles. Carefully, he tightened the seat belt for landing; below him he could see the vast, tangled expanse of Jungle-land spreading out to the horizon. Miles ahead was the bright circle of the landing field and the sparkling glow of the city beyond. Ravdin peered to the north of the city, hoping to catch a glimpse of the concert before his ship was swallowed by the brilliant landing lights.

A bell chimed softly in his ear. Ravdin forced his attention back to the landing operation. He was still numb and shaken from the Warp-passage, his mind still muddled by the abrupt and incredible change. Moments before, the sky had been a vast, starry blanket of black velvet; then, abruptly, he had been hovering over the city, sliding down toward warm friendly lights and music. He checked the proper switches, and felt the throbbing purr of the anti-grav motors as the ship slid in toward the landing slot. Tall spires of other ships rose to meet him, circle upon circle of silver needles pointing skyward. A little later they were blotted out as the ship was grappled into the berth from which it had risen days before.

With a sigh, Ravdin eased himself out of the seat, his heart pounding with excitement. Perhaps, he thought, he was too excited, too eager to be home, for his mind was still reeling from the fearful discovery of his journey.

The station was completely empty as Ravdin walked down the ramp to the shuttles. At the desk he checked in with the shiny punch-card robot, and walked swiftly across the polished floor. The wall panels pulsed a somber blue-green, broken sharply by brilliant flashes and overtones of scarlet, reflecting with subtle accuracy the tumult in his own mind. Not a sound was in the air, not a whisper nor sign of human habitation. Vaguely, uneasiness grew in his mind as he entered the shuttle station.

THE LINK

Suddenly, the music caught him, a long, low chord of indescribable beauty, rising and falling in the wind, a distant whisper of life....

The concert, of course. Everyone would be at the concert tonight, and even from two miles away, the beauty of four hundred perfectly harmonized voices was carried on the breeze. Ravdin's uneasiness disappeared; he was eager to discharge his horrible news, get it off his mind and join the others in the great amphitheater set deep in the hillside outside the city. But he knew instinctively that Lord Nehmon, anticipating his return, would not be at the concert.

Riding the shuttle over the edges of Jungle-land toward the shining bright beauty of the city, Ravdin settled back, trying to clear his mind of the shock and horror he had encountered on his journey. The curves and spires of glowing plastic passed him, lighted with a million hues. He realized that his whole life was entangled in the very beauty of this wonderful city. Everything he had ever hoped or dreamed lay sheltered here in the ever-changing rhythm of colors and shapes and sounds. And now, he knew, he would soon see his beloved city burning once again, turning to flames and ashes in a heart-breaking memorial to the age-old fear of his people.

The little shuttle-car settled down softly on the green terrace near the center of the city. The building was a masterpiece of smoothly curving walls and tasteful lines, opening a full side to the south to catch the soft sunlight and warm breezes. Ravdin strode across the deep carpeting of the terrace. There was other music here, different music, a wilder, more intimate fantasy of whirling sound. An oval door opened for him, and he stopped short, staggered for a moment by the overpowering beauty in the vaulted room.

A girl with red hair the color of new flame was dancing with enthralling beauty and abandon, her body moving like ripples

6

of wind to the music which filled the room with its throbbing cry. Her beauty was exquisite, every motion, every flowing turn a symphony of flawless perfection as she danced to the wild music.

"Lord Nehmon!"

The dancer threw back her head sharply, eyes wide, her body frozen in mid-air, and then, abruptly, she was gone, leaving only the barest flickering image of her fiery hair. The music slowed, singing softly, and Ravdin could see the old man waiting in the room. Nehmon rose, his gaunt face and graying hair belying the youthful movement of his body. Smiling, he came forward, clapped Ravdin on the shoulder, and took his hand warmly. "You're too late for the concert—it's a shame. Mischana is the master tonight, and the whole city is there."

Ravdin's throat tightened as he tried to smile. "I had to let you know," he said. "*They're coming*, Nehmon! I saw them, hours ago."

The last overtones of the music broke abruptly, like a glass shattered on stone. The room was deathly still. Lord Nehmon searched the young man's face. Then he turned away, not quite concealing the sadness and pain in his eyes. "You're certain? You couldn't be mistaken?"

"No chance. I found signs of their passing in a dozen places. Then I saw *them*, their whole fleet. There were hundreds. They're coming, I saw them."

"Did they see you?" Nehmon's voice was sharp.

"No, no. The Warp is a wonderful thing. With it I could come and go in the twinkling of an eye. But I could see them in the twinkling of an eye."

"And it couldn't have been anyone else?"

"Could anyone else build ships like the Hunters?"

THE LINK

Nehmon sighed wearily. "No one that we know." He glanced up at the young man. "Sit down, son, sit down. I—I'll just have to rearrange my thinking a little. Where were they? How far?"

"Seven light years," Ravdin said. "Can you imagine it? Just seven, and moving straight this way. *They know where we are, and they are coming quickly.*" His eyes filled with fear. "They *couldn't* have found us so soon, unless they too have discovered the Warp and how to use it to travel."

The older man's breath cut off sharply, and there was real alarm in his eyes. "You're right," he said softly. "Six months ago it was eight hundred light years away, in an area completely remote from us. Now just *seven*. In six months they have come so close."

The scout looked up at Nehmon in desperation. "But what can we do? We have only weeks, maybe days, before they're here. We have no time to plan, no time to prepare for them. What can we do?"

The room was silent. Finally the aged leader stood up, wearily, some fraction of his six hundred years of life showing in his face for the first time in centuries. "We can do once again what we always have done before when the Hunters came," he said sadly. "We can run away."

*

The bright street below the oval window was empty and quiet. Not a breath of air stirred in the city. Ravdin stared out in bitter silence. "Yes, we can run away. Just as we always have before. After we have worked so hard, accomplished so much here, we must burn the city and flee again." His voice trailed off to silence. He stared at Nehmon, seeking in the old man's face some answer, some reassurance. But he found no answer there, only sadness. "Think of the concerts. It's taken so long, but at last we've come so close to the ultimate goal." He gestured toward the thought-sensitive sounding boards lining the walls,

8

the panels which had made the dancer-illusion possible. "Think of the beauty and peace we've found here."

"I know. How well I know."

"Yet now the Hunters come again, and again we must run away." Ravdin stared at the old man, his eyes suddenly bright. "Nehmon, when I saw those ships I began thinking."

"I've spent many years thinking, my son."

"Not what I've been thinking." Ravdin sat down, clasping his hands in excitement. "The Hunters come and we run away, Nehmon. Think about that for a moment. We run, and we run, and we run. From what? We run from the Hunters. They're hunting *us*, these Hunters. They've never quite found us, because we've always already run. We're clever, we're fortunate, and we have a way of life that they do not, so whenever they have come close to finding us, we have run."

Nehmon nodded slowly. "For thousands of years."

Ravdin's eyes were bright. "Yes, we flee, we cringe, we hide under stones, we break up our lives and uproot our families, running like frightened animals in the shadows of night and secrecy." He gulped a breath, and his eyes sought Nehmon's angrily. "*Why do we run, my lord?*"

Nehmon's eyes widened. "Because we have no choice," he said. "We must run or be killed. You know that. You've seen the records, you've been taught."

"Oh, yes, I know what I've been taught. I've been taught that eons ago our remote ancestors fought the Hunters, and lost, and fled, and were pursued. But why do we keep running? Time after time we've been cornered, and we've turned and fled. *Why?* Even animals know that when they're cornered they must turn and fight."

"We are not animals." Nehmon's voice cut the air like a whiplash.

"But we could fight."

9

THE LINK

"Animals fight. We do not. We fought once, like animals, and now we must run from the Hunters who continue to fight like animals. So be it. Let the Hunters fight."

Ravdin shook his head. "Do you mean that the Hunters are not men like us?" he said. "That's what you're saying, that they are animals. All right. We kill animals for our food, isn't that true? We kill the tiger-beasts in the Jungle to protect ourselves, why not kill the Hunters to protect ourselves?"

Nehmon sighed, and reached out a hand to the young man. "I'm sorry," he said gently. "It seems logical, but it's false logic. The Hunters are men just like you and me. Their lives are different, their culture is different, but they are men. And human life is sacred, to us, above all else. This is the fundamental basis of our very existence. Without it we would be Hunters, too. If we fight, we are dead even if we live. That's why we must run away now, and always. Because we know that we must not kill men."

*

On the street below, the night air was suddenly full of voices, chattering, intermingled with whispers of song and occasional brief harmonic flutterings. The footfalls were muted on the polished pavement as the people passed slowly, their voices carrying a hint of puzzled uneasiness.

"The concert's over!" Ravdin walked to the window, feeling a chill pass through him. "So soon, I wonder why?" Eagerly he searched the faces passing in the street for Dana's face, sensing the lurking discord in the quiet talk of the crowd. Suddenly the sound-boards in the room tinkled a carillon of ruby tones in his ear, and she was in the room, rushing into his arms with a happy cry, pressing her soft cheek to his rough chin. "You're back! Oh, I'm so glad, so very glad!" She turned to the old man. "Nehmon, what has happened? The concert was ruined tonight.

10

There was something in the air, everybody felt it. For some reason the people seemed *afraid*."

Ravdin turned away from his bride. "Tell her," he said to the old man.

Dana looked at them, her gray eyes widening in horror. "The Hunters! They've found us?"

Ravdin nodded wordlessly.

Her hands trembled as she sat down, and there were tears in her eyes. "We came so close tonight, so very close. I *felt* the music before it was sung, do you realize that? I *felt* the fear around me, even though no one said a word. It wasn't vague or fuzzy, it was *clear*! The transference was perfect." She turned to face the old man. "It's taken so long to come this far, Nehmon. So much work, so much training to reach a perfect communal concert. We've had only two hundred years here, only *two hundred*! I was just a little girl when we came, I can't even remember before that. Before we came here we were undisturbed for a thousand years, and before that, four thousand. But *two hundred*—we *can't* leave now. Not when we've come so far."

Ravdin nodded. "That's the trouble. They come closer every time. This time they will catch us. Or the next time, or the next. And that will be the end of everything for us, unless we fight them." He paused, watching the last groups dispersing on the street below. "If we only knew, for certain, what we were running from."

There was a startled silence. The girl's breath came in a gasp and her eyes widened as his words sank home. "Ravdin," she said softly, "*have you ever seen a Hunter?*"

Ravdin stared at her, and felt a chill of excitement. Music burst from the sounding-board, odd, wild music, suddenly hopeful. "No," he said, "no, of course not. You know that."

The girl rose from her seat. "Nor have I. Never, not once." She turned to Lord Nehmon. "Have *you*?"

THE LINK

"Never." The old man's voice was harsh.

"Has *anyone* ever seen a Hunter?"

Ravdin's hand trembled. "I—I don't know. None of us living now, no. It's been too long since they last actually found us. I've read—oh, I can't remember. I think my grandfather saw them, or my great-grandfather, somewhere back there. It's been thousands of years."

"Yet we've been tearing ourselves up by the roots, fleeing from planet to planet, running and dying and still running. But suppose we don't need to run anymore?"

He stared at her. "They keep coming. They keep searching for us. What more proof do you need?"

Dana's face glowed with excitement, alive with new vitality, new hope. "Ravdin, can't you see? *They might have changed.* They might not be the same. Things can happen. Look at us, how we've grown since the wars with the Hunters. Think how our philosophy and culture have matured! Oh, Ravdin, you were to be master at a concert next month. Think how the concerts have changed! Even my grandmother can remember when the concerts were just a few performers playing, and everyone else just sitting and *listening*! Can you imagine anything more silly? They hadn't even thought of transference then, they never dreamed what a *real* concert could be! Why, those people had never begun to understand music until they themselves became a part of it. Even we can see these changes, why couldn't the Hunters have grown and changed just as we have?"

Nehmon's voice broke in, almost harshly, as he faced the excited pair. "The Hunters don't have concerts," he said grimly. "You're deluding yourself, Dana. They laugh at our music, they scoff at our arts and twist them into obscene mockeries. They have no concept of beauty in their language. The Hunters are incapable of change."

"And you can be certain of that when *nobody has seen them for thousands of years?*"

Nehmon met her steady eyes, read the strength and determination there. He knew, despairingly, what she was thinking—that he was old, that he couldn't understand, that his mind was channeled now beyond the approach of wisdom. "You mustn't think what you're thinking," he said weakly. "You'd be blind. You wouldn't know, you couldn't have any idea what you would find. If you tried to contact them, you could be lost completely, tortured, killed. If they haven't changed, you wouldn't stand a chance. You'd never come back, Dana."

"But she's right all the same," Ravdin said softly. "You're wrong, my lord. We can't continue this way if we're to survive. Sometime our people must contact them, find the link that was once between us, and forge it strong again. We could do it, Dana and I."

"I could forbid you to go."

Dana looked at her husband, and her eyes were proud. "You could forbid us," she said, facing the old man. "But you could never stop us."

*

At the edge of the Jungle-land a great beast stood with green-gleaming eyes, licking his fanged jaws as he watched the glowing city, sensing somehow that the mystifying circle of light and motion was soon to become his Jungle-land again. In the city the turmoil bubbled over, as wave after wave of the people made the short safari across the intervening jungle to the circles of their ships. Husbands, wives, fathers, mothers—all carried their small, frail remembrances out to the ships. There was music among them still, but it was a different sort of music, now, an eerie, hopeless music that drifted out of the city in the wind. It caused all but the bravest of the beasts, their hair prickling on their backs, to run in panic through the jungle

13

darkness. It was a melancholy music, carried from thought to thought, from voice to voice as the people of the city wearily prepared themselves once again for the long journey.

To run away. In the darkness of secrecy, to be gone, without a trace, without symbol or vestige of their presence, leaving only the scorched circle of land for the jungle to reclaim, so that no eyes, not even the sharpest, would ever know how long they had stayed, nor where they might have gone.

In the rounded room of his house, Lord Nehmon dispatched the last of his belongings, a few remembrances, nothing more, because the space on the ships must take people, not remembrances, and he knew that the remembrances would bring only pain. All day Nehmon had supervised the loading, the intricate preparation, following plans laid down millennia before. He saw the libraries and records transported, mile upon endless mile of microfilm, carted to the ships prepared to carry them, stored until a new resting place was found. The history of a people was recorded on that film, a people once proud and strong, now equally proud, but dwindling in numbers as toll for the constant roving. A proud people, yet a people who would turn and run without thought, in a panic of age-old fear. They *had* to run, Nehmon knew, if they were to survive.

And with a blaze of anger in his heart, he almost hated the two young people waiting here with him for the last ship to be filled. For these two would not go.

It had been a long and painful night. He had pleaded and begged, tried to persuade them that there was no hope, that the very idea of remaining behind or trying to contact the Hunters was insane. Yet he knew *they* were sane, perhaps unwise, naive, but their decision had been reached, and they would not be shaken.

The day was almost gone as the last ships began to fill. Nehmon turned to Ravdin and Dana, his face lined and tired.

"You'll have to go soon," he said. "The city will be burned, of course, as always. You'll be left with food, and with weapons against the jungle. The Hunters will know that we've been here, but they'll not know when, nor where we have gone." He paused. "It will be up to you to see that they don't learn."

Dana shook her head. "We'll tell them nothing, unless it's safe for them to know."

"They'll question you, even torture you."

She smiled calmly. "Perhaps they won't. But as a last resort, we can blank out."

Nehmon's face went white. "You know there is no coming back, once you do that. You would never regain your memory. You must save it for a last resort."

Down below on the street the last groups of people were passing; the last sweet, eerie tones of the concert were rising in the gathering twilight. Soon the last families would have taken their refuge in the ships, waiting for Nehmon to trigger the fire bombs to ignite the beautiful city after the ships started on their voyage. The concerts were over; there would be long years of aimless wandering before another home could be found, another planet safe from the Hunters and their ships. Even then it would be more years before the concerts could again rise from their hearts and throats and minds, generations before they could begin work again toward the climactic expression of their heritage.

Ravdin felt the desolation in the people's minds, saw the utter hopelessness in the old man's face, and suddenly felt the pressure of despair. It was such a slender hope, so frail and so dangerous. He knew of the terrible fight, the war of his people against the Hunters, so many thousand years before. They had risen together, a common people, their home a single planet. And then, the gradual splitting of the nations, his own people living in peace, seeking the growth and beauty of the arts,

15

despising the bitterness and barrenness of hatred and killing—and the Hunters, under an iron heel of militarism, of government for the perpetuation of government, split farther and farther from them. It was an ever-widening split as the Hunters sneered and ridiculed, and then grew to hate Ravdin's people for all the things the Hunters were losing: peace, love, happiness. Ravdin knew of his people's slowly dawning awareness of the sanctity of life, shattered abruptly by the horrible wars, and then the centuries of fear and flight, hiding from the wrath of the Hunters' vengeance. His people had learned much in those long years. They had conquered disease. They had grown in strength as they dwindled in numbers. But now the end could be seen, crystal clear, the end of his people and a ghastly grave.

Nehmon's voice broke the silence. "If you must stay behind, then go now. The city will burn an hour after the count-down."

"We will be safe, outside the city." Dana gripped her husband's hand, trying to transmit to him some part of her strength and confidence. "Wish us the best, Nehmon. If a link can be forged, we will forge it."

"I wish you the best in everything." There were tears in the old man's eyes as he turned and left the room.

*

They stood in the Jungle-land, listening to the scurry of frightened animals, and shivering in the cool night air as the bright sparks of the ships' exhausts faded into the black starry sky. A man and a woman alone, speechless, watching, staring with awful longing into the skies as the bright rocket jets dwindled to specks and flickered out.

The city burned. Purple spumes of flame shot high into the air, throwing a ghastly light on the frightened Jungle-land. Spires of flame seemed to be seeking the stars with their fingers as the plastic walls and streets of the city hissed and shriveled, blackening, bubbling into a vanishing memory before their eyes. The flames shot high, carrying with them the last remnants of the city which had stood proud and tall an hour before. Then a silence fell, deathly, like the lifeless silence of a grave. Out of the silence, little whispering sounds of the Jungle-land crept to their ears, first frightened, then curious, then bolder and bolder as the wisps of grass and little animals ventured out and out toward the clearing where the city had stood. Bit by bit the Jungle-land gathered courage, and the clearing slowly, silently, began to disappear.

Days later new sparks of light appeared in the black sky. They grew to larger specks, then to flares, and finally settled to the earth as powerful, flaming jets.

They were squat, misshapen vessels, circling down like vultures, hissing, screeching, landing with a grinding crash in the tall thicket near the place where the city had stood. Ravdin's signal had guided them in, and the Hunters had seen them, standing on a hilltop above the demolished amphitheater. Men had come out of the ships, large men with cold faces and dull eyes, weapons strapped to their trim uniforms. The Hunters had blinked at them, unbelieving, with their weapons held at ready. Ravdin and Dana were seized and led to the flagship.

As they approached it, their hearts sank and they clasped hands to bolster their failing hope.

The leader of the Hunters looked up from his desk as they were thrust into his cabin. Frankle's face was a graven mask as he searched their faces dispassionately. The captives were pale and seemed to cringe from the pale interrogation light. "Chickens!" the Hunter snorted. "We have been hunting down chickens." His eyes turned to one of the guards. "They have been searched?"

"Of course, master."

"And questioned?"

17

THE LINK

The guard frowned. "Yes, sir. But their language is almost unintelligible."

"You've studied the basic tongues, haven't you?" Frankle's voice was as cold as his eyes.

"Of course, sir, but this is so different."

Frankle stared in contempt at the fair-skinned captives, fixing his eyes on them for a long moment. Finally he said, "Well?"

Ravdin glanced briefly at Dana's white face. His voice seemed weak and high-pitched in comparison to the Hunter's baritone. "You are the leader of the Hunters?"

Frankle regarded him sourly, without replying. His thin face was swarthy, his short-cut gray hair matching the cold gray of his eyes. It was an odd face, completely blank of any thought or emotion, yet capable of shifting to a strange biting slyness in the briefest instant. It was a rich face, a face of inscrutable depth. He pushed his chair back, his eyes watchful. "We know your people were here," he said suddenly. "Now they've gone, and yet you remain behind. There must be a reason for such rashness. Are you sick? Crippled?"

Ravdin shook his head. "We are not sick."

"Then criminals, perhaps? Being punished for rebellious plots?"

"We are not criminals."

The Hunter's fist crashed on the desk. "Then why are you here? *Why?* Are you going to tell me now, or do you propose to waste a few hours of my time first?"

"There is no mystery," Ravdin said softly. "We stayed behind to plead for peace."

"For peace?" Frankle stared in disbelief. Then he shrugged, his face tired. "I might have known. Peace! Where have your people gone?"

Ravdin met him eye for eye. "I can't say."

The Hunter laughed. "Let's be precise, you don't *choose* to say, just now. But perhaps very soon you will wish with all your heart to tell me."

Dana's voice was sharp. "We're telling you the truth. We want peace, nothing more. This constant hunting and running is senseless, exhausting to both of us. We want to make peace with you, to bring our people together again."

Frankle snorted. "You came to us in war, once, long ago. Now you want peace. What would you do, clasp us to your bosom, smother us in your idiotic music? Or have you gone on to greater things?"

Ravdin's face flushed hotly. "Much greater things," he snapped.

Frankle sat down slowly. "No doubt," he said. "Now understand me clearly. Very soon you will be killed. How quickly or slowly you die will depend largely upon the civility of your tongues. A civil tongue answers questions with the right answers. That is my definition of a civil tongue." He sat back coldly. "Now, shall we commence asking questions?"

Dana stepped forward suddenly, her cheeks flushed. "We don't have the words to express ourselves," she said softly. "We can't tell you in words what we have to say, but music is a language even you can understand. We can tell you what we want in music."

Frankle scowled. He knew about the magic of this music, he had heard of the witchcraft these weak chicken-people could weave, of their strange, magic power to steal strong men's minds from them and make them like children before wolves. But he had never heard this music with his own ears. He looked at them, his eyes strangely bright. "You know I cannot listen to your music. It is forbidden, even you should know that. How dare you propose—"

THE LINK

"But this is different music." Dana's eyes widened, and she threw an excited glance at her husband. "Our music is beautiful, wonderful to hear. If you could only hear it—"

"Never." The man hesitated. "Your music is forbidden, poisonous."

Her smile was like sweet wine, a smile that worked into the Hunter's mind like a gentle, lazy drug. "But who is to permit or forbid? After all, you are the leader here, and forbidden pleasures are all the sweeter."

Frankle's eyes were on hers, fascinated. Slowly, with a graceful movement, she drew the gleaming thought-sensitive stone from her clothing. It glowed in the room with a pearly luminescence, and she saw the man's eyes turning to it, drawn as if by magic. Then he looked away, and a cruel smile curled his lips. He motioned toward the stone. "All right," he said mockingly. "Do your worst. Show me your precious music."

Like a tinkle of glass breaking in a well, the stone flashed its fiery light in the room. Little swirls of music seemed to swell from it, blossoming in the silence. Frankle tensed, a chill running up his spine, his eyes drawn back to the gleaming jewel. Suddenly, the music filled the room, rising sweetly like an overpowering wave, filling his mind with strange and wonderful images. The stone shimmered and changed, taking the form of dancing clouds of light, swirling with the music as it rose. Frankle felt his mind groping toward the music, trying desperately to reach into the heart of it, to become part of it.

Ravdin and Dana stood there, trancelike, staring transfixed at the gleaming center of light, forcing their joined minds to create the crashing, majestic chords as the song lifted from the depths of oblivion to the heights of glory in the old, old song of their people.

A song of majesty, and strength, and dignity. A song of love, of aspiration, a song of achievement. A song of peoples driven

20

by ancient fears across the eons of space, seeking only peace, even peace with those who drove them.

Frankle heard the music, and could not comprehend, for his mind could not grasp the meaning, the true overtones of those glorious chords, but he felt the strangeness in the pangs of fear which groped through his mind, cringing from the wonderful strains, dazzled by the dancing light. He stared wide-eyed and trembling at the couple across the room, and for an instant it seemed that he was stripped naked. For a fleeting moment the authority was gone from his face; gone too was the cruelty, the avarice, the sardonic mockery. For the briefest moment his cold gray eyes grew incredibly tender with a sudden ancient, long-forgotten longing, crying at last to be heard.

And then, with a scream of rage he was stumbling into the midst of the light, lashing out wildly at the heart of its shimmering brilliance. His huge hand caught the hypnotic stone and swept it into crashing, ear-splitting cacophony against the cold steel bulkhead. He stood rigid, his whole body shaking, eyes blazing with fear and anger and hatred as he turned on Ravdin and Dana. His voice was a raging storm of bitterness drowning out the dying strains of the music.

"Spies! You thought you could steal my mind away, make me forget my duty and listen to your rotten, poisonous noise! Well, you failed, do you hear? I didn't hear it, I didn't listen, *I didn't*! I'll hunt you down as my fathers hunted you down, I'll bring my people their vengeance and glory, and your foul music will be dead!"

He turned to the guards, wildly, his hands still trembling. "Take them out! Whip them, burn them, do anything! But find out where their people have gone. Find out! Music! We'll take the music out of them, once and for all."

*

21

THE LINK

The inquisition had been horrible. Their minds had had no concept of such horror, such relentless, racking pain. The blazing lights, the questions screaming in their ears, Frankle's vicious eyes burning in frustration, and their own screams, rising with each question they would not answer until their throats were scorched and they could no longer scream. Finally they reached the limit they could endure, and muttered together the hoarse words that could deliver them. Not words that Frankle could hear, but words to bring deliverance, to blank out their minds like a wet sponge over slate. The hypnotic key clicked into the lock of their minds; their screams died in their brains. Frankle stared at them, and knew instantly what they had done, a technique of memory obliteration known and dreaded for so many thousands of years that history could not remember. As his captives stood mindless before him, he let out one hoarse, agonized scream of frustration and defeat.

But strangely enough he did not kill them. He left them on a cold stone ledge, blinking dumbly at each other as the ships of his fleet rose one by one and vanished like fireflies in the dark night sky. Naked, they sat alone on the planet of the Jungle-land. They knew no words, no music, nothing. And they did not even know that in the departing ships a seed had been planted. For Frankle *had* heard the music. He had grasped the beauty of his enemies for that brief instant, and in that instant they had become less his enemies. A tiny seed of doubt had been planted. The seed would grow.

The two sat dumbly, shivering. Far in the distance, a beast roared against the heavy night, and a light rain began to fall. They sat naked, the rain soaking their skin and hair. Then one of them grunted, and moved into the dry darkness of the cave. Deep within him some instinct spoke, warning him to fear the roar of the animal.

Blinking dully, the woman crept into the cave after him. Three thoughts alone filled their empty minds. Not thoughts of Nehmon and his people; to them, Nehmon had never existed, forgotten as completely as if he had never been. No thoughts of the Hunters, either, nor of their unheard-of mercy in leaving them their lives—lives of memoryless oblivion, like animals in this green Jungle-land, but lives nonetheless.

Only three thoughts filled their minds:

It was raining.

They were hungry.

The Saber-tooth was prowling tonight.

They never knew that the link had been forged.